Owen Kane
111 Chestnut Ave.
Libertyville, PA 19606

Granny Lewis
562 Marshall Ave.
Pennside, CA 91024

The Giant Hug

by Sandra Horning • illustrated by Valeri Gorbachev

Alfred A. Knopf New York

"What do you want to send Granny for her birthday?" Owen's mother asked.

"A GIANT hug," Owen replied. He opened his arms as wide as he possibly could to show how giant the hug would be.

"Do you want to draw a picture of you hugging Granny?" his mother asked.

"No," Owen said, "I want to send a real hug. I'll give the mailman a hug and ask him to send it to Granny."

They gathered their letters and walked to the post office in town.

Soon they got to the front of the line and Mr. Nevin called out, "Next!"

"I want to mail a hug to my granny. Will you please send it?" Owen asked in his most polite voice.

"Well, we don't normally send hugs, but I suppose we could give it a try," Mr. Nevin said.

Owen's mother wrote down Granny's address for Mr. Nevin.

Owen walked behind the counter, opened his arms as wide as he possibly could, and gave Mr. Nevin a giant hug.

"Please make the hug just as giant when you pass it to the mailman," Owen said.

"Oh, I won't see the mailman who delivers it to your granny. I give the mail to Ms. Porter, who sorts it and puts it on a truck to the big city. After that it's put on a plane and flown across the country," Mr. Nevin said.

"Well, you will have to hug Ms. Porter then," Owen said as
Mr. Nevin carried the mail to Ms. Porter.

Mr. Nevin looked down awkwardly at Ms. Porter as he handed her the mail and the address of Owen's granny. He blushed and mumbled, "And, uh, here's the hug."

Mr. Nevin opened his arms as wide as he possibly could and gave Ms. Porter a giant hug.

Ms. Porter smiled as she sorted the mail. Just then the driver came to collect the mail bound for the big city. As the driver lifted the last heavy bag of mail, Ms. Porter said, "Leroy, one more thing. Someone is sending a hug to his granny. Here is the address, and here is the hug."

Ms. Porter opened her arms as wide as she possibly could and gave Leroy a giant hug.

Leroy laughed and said, "Now that's a piece of mail you don't see too often."

Leroy whistled on the way to the big city. After unloading the mail, he checked the schedule to see who was driving the mail to the airport. It read "James." Leroy found James in the break room eating his morning snack.

"Hi, James. I know this seems a little odd, but a hug is being sent through the mail to someone's granny and this is her address," Leroy said.

Leroy opened his arms as wide as he possibly could and gave James a giant hug.
James cringed. He was not the hugging type, but he would do his job.

Later that afternoon James arrived at the airport. He asked a
mail handler when the mail was being loaded onto the plane.
   "That mail was taken to the plane a few minutes ago," the mail
handler said.

   James rushed to the plane, where Captain Johnson was getting
ready to board.
   "Captain, a kid is sending a hug through the mail to his granny.
Here is the address, and here is the hug," James said with a grimace.

James opened his arms as wide as he possibly could and
gave Captain Johnson a giant hug.
"Now isn't that a grand way to start the day!"
Captain Johnson bellowed.

When the plane landed, Captain Johnson walked to the airport post office.

He saw Amanda standing next to a mail truck, looking sad.

"Hello. Are you driving the truck to the city?" Captain Johnson asked.

Amanda nodded glumly.

"A hug is being sent through the mail," Captain Johnson announced.

Captain Johnson opened his arms as wide as he possibly could and gave Amanda a giant hug.

Amanda brightened and said, "Thank you."

She bobbed her head to the music as she drove.
After unloading the mail, Amanda went to find Chad,
the driver taking the mail to Granny's town.

"Chad, a hug is being sent through the mail. Here is the address, and, well, here's the hug," Amanda said as her face turned red.

Amanda opened her arms as wide as she possibly could and gave Chad a giant hug.

Chad chuckled and said, "Finally! Do you want to go dancing tonight?"

"I'd love to!" Amanda exclaimed.

Chad kicked up his heels and hopped in his truck. Early
the next morning Chad drove to Granny's town.

As he prepared to return to the city, he remembered the hug.
"Who will be delivering the mail to Pennside today?" Chad
asked the supervisor.

"Shelly, but she's not here yet," Ms. Greenberg replied as
she adjusted her glasses.

"Please pass this along to her," Chad said.

Chad opened his arms as wide as he possibly could and gave
Ms. Greenberg a giant hug.

Ms. Greenberg gasped with surprise and her glasses tilted to the side.

"Shelly, I need a word with you," Ms. Greenberg called when Shelly arrived.

"A hug is being sent through the mail to a boy's granny and you are the mailwoman delivering it," Ms. Greenberg said.

Ms. Greenberg opened her arms as wide as she possibly could and gave Shelly a giant hug.

"Granny will be delighted!" Shelly exclaimed.

Shelly stopped to smell the flowers as she delivered mail from door to door. She saw Granny gardening in the yard.

"Ms. Lewis, I have a special delivery for you," Shelly said. "Your grandson has sent you a hug."

Shelly opened her arms as wide as she possibly could
and gave Granny a giant hug.

Granny grinned and said, "That's the most wonderful piece of mail I have ever received. You send that grandson of mine a big kiss."

Granny puckered up her lips and gave Shelly a big, wet kiss on the cheek.

For my mom and dad, and thanks to
Brendan, Eoin, and Gavin—SH

I'm sending my giant hug to all my friends
who are far away—VG

THIS IS A BORZOI BOOK PUBLISHED BY ALFRED A. KNOPF

Text copyright © 2005 by Sandra Horning
Illustrations copyright © 2005 by Valeri Gorbachev
All rights reserved under International and Pan-American Copyright Conventions.
Published in the United States by Alfred A. Knopf, an imprint of Random House Children's Books,
a division of Random House, Inc., New York, and simultaneously in Canada by Random House of
Canada Limited, Toronto. Distributed by Random House, Inc., New York.
KNOPF, BORZOI BOOKS, and the colophon are registered trademarks
of Random House, Inc.

www.randomhouse.com/kids

Library of Congress Cataloging-in-Publication Data
Horning, Sandra.
The giant hug / by Sandra Horning ; illustrated by Valeri Gorbachev. — 1st ed.
p. cm.
SUMMARY: When Owen sends a real hug to his grandmother for her birthday, he inadvertently
brings cheer to the postal workers as they pass the hug along.
ISBN 0-375-82477-4 (trade) — ISBN 0-375-92477-9 (lib. bdg.)
[1. Hugging—Fiction. 2. Postal service—Fiction. 3. Grandmothers—Fiction.]
I. Gorbachev, Valeri, ill. II. Title.
PZ7.H7867Gi 2005
[E]—dc22
2003025883

MANUFACTURED IN CHINA
January 2005
10 9 8 7 6 5
First Edition

20c

37c

37c

20c

20c

20c

50c

50c

37c

50c